# Frazzled

Super Mum book one

I0591853

## Stacey Broadbent

Published by Stacey Broadbent
Copyright © 2021 Stacey Broadbent

Second edition

Originally published as Super Mum? From One Frazzled Mum to
Another in 2016

Licence Notes

Proofreading by Spell Bound
Cover design by Stacey Broadbent
Cover images from Deposit Photos


ISBN:    978-0-473-57170-2 (paperback)
         978-0-473-57171-9 (MOBI)

For all those sleep-deprived, frazzled mothers out there, who are doing the best they can.

# Contents

**Frazzled**

# The Test

**Waiting** for those two pink lines on a pee stick, is always a mixture of eager anticipation, nervousness and, above all else, hope. It doesn't matter whether it was planned, or accidental, there is always hope.

In this instance, it was purely accidental. And even though my husband and I had decided together, after child number three (the difficult one), that there would be no more, I find myself here, knickers around my ankles, sitting on the throne, trying not to look at the stick for fear of jinxing it, secretly hoping for a positive.

Yep. That's me.

Realistically, I know that another baby would add to my already super high stress levels, but that still doesn't stop me from wishing for it to happen. You see, when I was growing up, the one thing I was certain of in life, was that I wanted to be a mother. More than anything in the world, that was what I wanted. I couldn't decide on a career choice, but motherhood was one thing I was sure I was destined for.

Not just your standard 2.4 children either. I wanted four kids; it had to be even numbers so that no-one was

# Frazzled

left out, and it had to be more than two, because my sister and I had always longed for another sibling. So four, was my magic number.

Making the decision to stop after three was a hard one for me. Like I said though, child number three was particularly challenging, and sleep was hard to come by. Making babies wasn't exactly high on my list.

One year later, and I'm several days late.

I'm *never* late.

After the first day, I panicked, wondering how hubby would respond to the news that perhaps there could be another bundle of joy for us. On day two, I was quietly confident that there was indeed a little person growing inside of me, and I couldn't be happier. Day three, I started planning out how we would arrange the rooms of our small three-bedroom home to fit in another person.

This is what I do. It's how my brain works. I plan things out. I'm not ashamed to admit I'm a bit of a control freak. I write mental lists all day, every day. They keep me up at night sometimes too. I'm weird like that.

Anyway, I digress.

I look at that pee stick.

One solitary line stares back at me.

It's negative.

I am both heartbroken and relieved all at once. My heart still yearns for one more baby.

Just one more.

My mind, on the other hand, knows deep down that this is for the best for my sanity's sake. Three

# Frazzled

children is already a handful, and they like to keep me on my toes each and every day. Adding another to the mix would be plain crazy.

Allow me to run you through a recent scenario in our household to prove that point:

"Sweetheart, can you please get dressed so we can go do the groceries?"
"Yip!"

*Five minutes later...*

"Are you dressed yet?"
"No."

*I go to investigate and Zoe (child three), is lying naked on the floor, building a castle with her blocks.*

"Remember when I said we were going to get the groceries? Well you need to get dressed so we can go."
"Okay."

*Five minutes later...*

"Time to go!"
"But I'm not dressed yet!"

*sigh*

# Frazzled

Now this conversation happens Every. Single. Week. More than once, in fact, just substitute groceries, with preschool/grandma's/town.

Back to the story…

*They finally emerge, clutching each other's hands, wearing mismatched, stained clothes, one gumboot and one jandal each, and their hair, a tangled mess. They grin and run out to the car. These are my kids.*

*Yes, I know I could make them change into tidy clothes, and if it's important, I will, but on ordinary days, it really isn't worth the fifteen-minute argument, so yes, I let my children wear whatever they want. Even if it looks like we live on the street.*

*Cut to the grocery store, and we go over the rules before getting out of the car:*

"No running, no screaming, no arguing, no asking for things, keep your hands to yourself."

*Before we even get into the store, Zoe trips over her own feet and falls to the ground. Her skirt flies up and reveals… a bare bottom! Embarrassing much?!*

*Never, in all the scenarios in my head of what motherhood would be like, did I envisage having to remind my child to put knickers on. Alas, this is a recurrent theme for us.*

*I hastily pick her up, glancing behind me to make sure no-one is watching, and dust her off. We proceed with our shopping expedition.*

# Frazzled

*Zoe is seated in the trolley, while Ellie (child two), is walking beside me.*

*That peace lasts for all of two minutes:*

"Mum! Can I have cherries?"

"No, honey, we're not getting cherries today."

"But I like cherries."

"I like cherries too, but they're expensive, and we're not doing a big shop today."

"But I want them."

"I know, but I said we're not getting them."

"But *I LIKE THEM*!"

*Meanwhile, Ellie is bored of walking nicely beside me, and has started to weave in and out of the other trolleys.*

*By some miracle we make it through the next aisle unscathed, only to have an argument break out about the notebook that the girls are now looking after for me. Both are sitting in the trolley now, and both want to hold the notebook. I give them each a piece of paper and put the notebook back into my bag.*

*Zoe is not happy with this arrangement:*

"But I wanted to hold the list!"

"I know you did, but you were ripping the pages out. You still have your own list though."

"But I wanted *THAT* one!"

"Well, you're not having that one. Sit down please."

# Frazzled

"I'm being good, aren't I, Mummy?" *a smug Ellie asks from her perch in the trolley.*

"Yes, Ellie, you are being good, thank you."

*This is when the crying begins (Zoe, not me, though it's tempting). Not quiet crying either, the kind where she throws her head back and cries from the back of her throat, all the while yelling that she wanted to hold the list.*

*I pick up the pace, desperate to get out of the store before someone kicks us out for disturbing the peace. I try reminding her that she is allowed to have one of her lollies when we get home if she is good, and this behaviour isn't acceptable. She stops and sniffs. She looks down at the piece of paper in her hand.*

"I…really   *sniff*   wanted   *sniff*   to   hold the…*LIST!*"

*More wailing.*

*I finally make it through the checkout, albeit frazzled. We make our way out to the car and Zoe starts asking for her lolly.*

*I tell her that she didn't follow the rules so she wouldn't be allowed to get her lolly.*

*Cue more wailing.*

*After the short, but extremely loud, drive home, I quietly open the car door, unbuckle her seat and take*

# Frazzled

*her by the hand. I lead her to the bedroom and tell her that she can come out when she has stopped crying and is ready to behave. I close the door, taking a deep breath to calm down.*

"I want to come out!" *She bangs on the door with her little fists.*

"You need to calm down, and then you can come out and join us."

"*I AM CALM!*"

"No, you're not. You're yelling, so you are not calm. When you have calmed down, then you can come out."

"*I AM CALM! I HAVE STOPPED!*"

"Yelling at me that you are calm, is not being calm. Just stop crying and you can come out."

*It goes quiet for 20 seconds.*

"*I STOPPED!! I AM CALM!!*"

"When you have stopped and I can tell that you are calm, then you can come back out."

*By now I am getting really agitated.*
*It's a simple request!*

*More banging on the door.*

*I give in. I open the door.*

# Frazzled

*Zoe is lying on the floor, one foot lifted, ready to kick the door once again. Her face is red and she has tears in her eyes.*

"Would you like a cuddle?" *I ask.*

"Yu-huh." *She flings her little arms around my neck. All the tension goes out of my body with the feeling of those chubby arms wrapped around me. She snuffles and buries her head in my chest.*

*I melt.*

"I love you," *I say.*

"I…love…you…too" *she murmurs through her sniffs.*

That right there? That is what makes me want another. Crazy, right?

# The Plan

**Unfortunately**, as I mentioned earlier, hubby is more than happy with our small tribe of three and isn't all that keen on a fourth. Thus, I must change his mind.

This, of course, requires a plan *(told you I like plans)*. I need to be smart about this. What are the reasons he has for not wanting any more children?

a) Probably the biggest obstacle is our financial situation. Things are a little tight for us right now. And by tight, I mean we are budgeted to the very last dollar each week, leaving no money whatsoever for saving. I mean, all our credit cards are maxed out to the limits. Okay, so we may be bordering on bankruptcy, but let's not focus on that. Alright? Good.

b) The next problem, which theoretically falls under the financial hardship category, is our home. Don't get me wrong, I love our home, but it's not exactly huge. There are only three bedrooms, and with the girls sharing one, Devon—our oldest—in his own room, and then, of course, us in ours, that doesn't exactly leave anywhere for baby number four and all the paraphernalia that goes along with said baby.

c)  There is also the topic of my sanity (*see last chapter*), but let's not go there, shall we? Moving right along.

d)  The other minor issue is that Zoe (*a.k.a devil child*) still likes to climb into our bed most nights. As you can imagine, this does not make for a good night's sleep (*did I mention my sanity already?*). This also forms a problem in that the whole baby making process is nigh on impossible in this situation. Alone time? Don't be daft.

Now that I have my list, I have to come up with a solution.

Clearly the money is the biggest issue—*I mean, it takes up two points on my list*—so this is what I should work on first…

**A** few days later, I find myself curled in the foetal position at the bottom of the bed, whilst Zoe is 'starfished' across my pillow, and hubby lays completely unaffected by what was quite obviously an eventful night for me. I sneak out into the lounge to ponder my predicament.

Money.

Hubby already works full time, so to get *more* money would require *me* to add another job to my bow. I need to find something that can fit in and around my other part-time job, my home duties, and, of course, the children.

Piece of cake.

I sit at my desk, flicking through an Avon catalogue that Granny dropped off the day before, while at the same time perusing the internet. I Google such things as "Work from home" and "How to become a millionaire overnight" when it hits me!

Why didn't I think of it sooner?

I could be an Avon rep like Granny! The hours are flexible, making it the perfect job opportunity for me.

When it is an acceptable hour, I call her and tell her of my plan. Happy to have one of her granddaughters follow in her footsteps, she invites me to a conference that evening with all the big-wigs, and I get so caught up in their enthusiasm, that I sign up right then and there. They make it sound so simple!

Which it probably is if you're actually into make-up. Which I am not. I don't now, nor have I ever, worn a lot of make-up. So when people ask me questions about the products, I have no idea what to tell them! I mean, they're talking to a girl (*and I use that term loosely*) who doesn't use any kind of cleanser/toner regime—just good old water and a face cloth for this gal. This makes me a tiny bit flustered.

# Frazzled

Which brings me to the other tiny flaw that my brain neglected to remind me of; I am not a saleswoman. I was not born with the 'gift of the gab' so to speak. I'm not an overly confident person, which is kind of an important trait to have when your job requires that you approach people and try to convince them they need what you're selling.

Let me paint you a little picture.

You know that awkward person at parties who gravitates to the corner where all the food is? That's me. While everyone else is mingling and enjoying themselves, I'm stuffing my face with an entire tray of canapes, trying to suss out who is the safest bet to strike up a conversation with. Will it be the slurring drunk at the bar? The group of cackling women across the room? The hippy-esque dancer on the dancefloor who is in their own little world? Who is less likely to laugh at me if I say something stupid? Who looks as though they could happily carry a conversation without my having to input much at all?

It's not as if I have nothing interesting to say; I mean, I think I'm as interesting as the next person, I just have trouble making the words in my head come out of my mouth. It's like every knowledgeable piece of information I have has somehow escaped me, and I can't manage to string a simple sentence together. I don't appear to have the 'small talk' gene. I think it skipped me and went straight to my sister—now that

# Frazzled

girl is *never* lost for words. I wish I could be more like her, but I'm not. I am me.

I don't even know where this irrational fear came from. It's not as though there was some traumatic event that scarred me for life.

Nope. As far as I can remember, I've always been this way. I have this overwhelming desire to be liked by everyone. I don't know that that's a bad thing, but it can be rather exhausting.

Look at me, digressing again.
Back to the story…

My representative start-up pack arrives, and I dive straight in, excited to start making loads of money (yes, I *am* that naïve). I get to work putting my details on the back of all the catalogues, ready for delivery. I see that they have given me the small area around my house, which makes it nice and easy to walk around with the children.

Jackets zipped and gloves on, we make our way out the door to begin the money-making adventure.

Four houses down and Zoe is tired and doesn't want to walk anymore. I hoist her into my arms, juggling the bag of catalogues to my other shoulder. Ellie skips along beside me, keeping up a constant babble.

"Look, Mum, I found a leaf! Ooh look! A flower! Can you hold these for me? I want to find more things." She grins, and I can't help but agree. I find a small space in my bag to squeeze her findings and we carry on with our walk.

"Mum! Look! A balloon!" she suddenly shrieks, excitement all over her face as she gallops towards it.

She's bending over, her tiny fingers within grasping reach when I realise exactly what this 'balloon' is.

"Don't touch that! It's not a balloon, honey." I grab her hand and shuffle her past, cringing and silently cursing the heathens that thought the footpath was an appropriate place to discard of their 'contraceptive device'.

"I want a balloon though." She stamps her feet stubbornly.

"I know, darling, but like I said, that isn't a balloon. I'll see if I can find you one when we get home."

We reach the end of the street and now Ellie is dragging her feet.

"I'm thirsty, can we stop now?"

"I'm hunggggrrrreeee!" Zoe adds.

"We only have a little bit more to do, you can have something to eat and drink when we get back."

"But I'm tiiiiiirrrrrreeedddddd!" Ellie whines. "Can you carry me?"

I look at her. I look at Zoe.

I sigh.

"Sure, sweetheart. I'll just deliver the rest of these later." I manoeuvre my bag so it's resting on my back. I sit Zoe up a little higher and then bend on an extremely awkward angle to lift Ellie onto my other hip. I now look like a pack horse. It's a good thing I have ample thighs and hips!

I trudge back towards our home, the bag bouncing against my back with every step. I can feel Ellie slipping further down, so I attempt to throw her up a smidge higher on my hip, which in turn makes the bag fall down to the crook of my elbow, and it is now swinging against the back of my knee. I feel myself slowing down under the weight, my arms threatening to give way. The shakes begin and sweat pours down my face—I know what you're thinking, hot, right?

By the time we get to our house, I'm walking with my legs wide apart—as if I've been riding horseback— when in actual fact, it's to help with keeping the kids from sliding further. As it is, they are barely within my grip. Their bare tummies and backs are exposed to the cool air as my hands clutch at their jackets in an attempt to keep them in my arms, and to top it off, I can feel a bruise forming behind my knee from the constant hammering of the bag of catalogues.

All in all, a fun-filled experience for everyone.

# The Revised Plan

**Five-thirty**, and I wake to the smiling face of Zoe and her very well-loved, stuffed giraffe. She waves him in my face. "It's morning time!" she chimes, full of the energy only a three-year-old can muster at this ungodly hour.

"Mmmhmmm," I mumble incoherently, throwing the blankets back for her to climb in. She snuggles down, and I plant a kiss on her nose. "Sleep," I whisper, stroking my fingers down her eyelids, willing them to close.

"But it's morning time! I want porridge!"

I sigh. Generally speaking, I'm a damn good cook, but porridge is my nemesis. For some reason, I lack the skills to make it creamy and smooth like my husband has perfected. Instead, it always ends up a lumpy blob of gruel. Very unappealing. And yet, my children insist on asking me to make it, even though they know I'm not good at it and they prefer Dad's. I don't really understand their logic, but I play along with the charade anyway.

"It's a preschool morning, remember? Mummy doesn't make porridge on those days. Daddy will make it in the weekend, okay?"

# Frazzled

"But I really want porridge." She pouts.

"Yes, I know, but we don't have time on these mornings, remember? Daddy will make it when he is home," I try again.

There is a moment of silence as she gathers her breath, and I brace myself for the explosion.

It begins as a high-pitched squeal, turning into a long, drawn-out wail. She kicks her feet and balls her little fists. If it weren't so early in the morning, it would almost be funny. Almost.

"Shhh! You will wake your brother and sister." She sucks in another breath, ready to let loose again. "Ah fine!" I roll out of bed and trudge begrudgingly to the kitchen. She skips behind me, a huge smile on her face. "Choose your bowl and put it on the bench," I say.

*side note* *You know that saying, "Hell hath no fury like a woman scorned"? I think it should be changed to "Hell hath no fury like a toddler who wanted the orange plate, not the green one." The number of arguments over the colour of a plate/fork/spoon/cup that I have witnessed! I have learned to just let them pick their own – less stress.*

I pour the oats into the saucepan and mix with a little water to make a paste like my husband has shown me. I add more water and put it on the heat, stirring. So far, so good. I carry on stirring, keeping a steady eye on the pot, and in a matter of seconds, as per usual, the lumps start appearing. No amount of beating makes them go away.

# Frazzled

I spoon the thick blobs into their bowls, adding a splash of milk and a swirl of golden syrup to attempt to make it look more appealing.

I go and make the beds and put on a load of washing, flicking the jug on on my way past. I open the curtains and put the girls' clothes away in their drawers for them, then go to make my coffee. Zoe is pushing her bowl away, having eaten the golden syrup off the top and not really touching the porridge. She folds her arms across her chest, a scowl on her face.

"I don't want it," she says defiantly. "I wanted pancakes."

"Then why did you ask for porridge?"

"I didn't! I asked for pancakes!"

"No, you asked for porridge."

"No, I didn't!"

"Yes, you did."

"No!"

"Fine. Don't eat it then. I'll put it in the bin. You can go and get dressed."

"But I'm hungry!"

"Then eat your breakfast."

We stare at each other, neither one willing to back down. Her hunger eventually gets the better of her, and she drags her bowl towards her and picks up the spoon, defeated. I turn back to my jobs, a smug smile on my face. Mum 1, Zoe 0.

# Frazzled

**Breakfast** done, and I sit down to look at my books and see how much money I've actually made over the last two months of my business endeavour. I stare at the figure in front of me in disbelief.

Surely not.

I pull out my phone and select the calculator app, punching the numbers in again. Yep. I was right the first time. I made a grand total of… minus one hundred and forty-eight dollars.

Minus one-hundred and forty-eight dollars.

*Minus one-hundred and forty-eight dollars!*

I had bought stock to have on hand; new products that I was sure would sell. Stock that was still sitting in my cupboard, unopened. The few sales I *had* made, hadn't even covered the things I had bought.

I dropped my head in my hands, wondering what I should do.

Zoe saunters across the room looking proud of herself, her hair wet and slicked back. I peer at her through the gap in my fingers.

"Why is your hair wet?" I ask, knowing I'm going to regret it.

"Because I wanted it to be smooth when I brushed it," she said matter-of-factly. That's not so bad.

"Where did you get the water from?" I ask, grabbing my coffee and hoping there isn't a mess of water all over the floor. She has a tendency to get facecloths sopping wet and then walk around washing her face, leaving a trail of water behind her. I can't fault her for trying to keep clean, but it'd be nice if it didn't create more work for me.

"The toilet," she says, as if it's the most normal thing in the world.

"What?" I splutter, nearly choking on my coffee.

"The toilet."

"You got the water from the toilet?" I demand.

"Ah-huh." She grins at me. "I swirled it in the toilet so it would be smooth."

"I hope you are joking," I say as I get up and walk into the bathroom. Sure enough, there is water around the toilet and on the seat. I edge closer, hoping to see an empty toilet bowl. I hang my head. "There is pee in the toilet," I say. "There is pee and toilet paper in there. Did you put your hair in there before or after you peed?" I ask.

"After."

*For the love of God, why?* "Why? Why would you do that? That's so gross, Zoe!"

"I wanted my hair to be smooth."

"I understand that, but why would you want wees in your hair? Get your clothes off, you have to have a shower now." I pull the curtain across and turn the shower on. I turn to flush the toilet and that is when I see a giant wad of toilet paper crumpled on the floor. "Why is there toilet paper on the floor?"

"I don't know," she says innocently, climbing into the shower.

# Frazzled

"Ellie!" I call out. "Ellie, come here!"

She skips into the bathroom. "What, Mummy?" she asks sweetly.

I point at the wad on the floor. "Did you do this?"

"Yes," she says, as if it should be obvious.

"Why? That's just wasting toilet paper."

"Because I needed something long and white and soft for a surprise for Zoe," she says. I stare at her, not really knowing what to say. She just stares right back. I shake my head, thankful that I will be sitting in my office at work soon. I might get a little peace there.

*I mean, what else could go wrong? Clearly, I'm not the money-maker I thought I could be, and my children need constant supervision.*

*Maybe adding another part-time job from home wasn't such a good idea. Maybe I'm going about this all wrong. Maybe I shouldn't focus on* making *money, but on* saving *it!*

*That's it! That's what I'll do!*

*How hard can it be?*

# Oh The Joys...

**Thud**, thud, thud, thud…

I peel one of my eyes open, squinting at the glowing red numbers of the alarm clock.

Two-forty-five in the morning!

I look to the end of the bed to find my three-year-old (complete with smelly giraffe), staring at me.

"What are you doing?" I whisper.

"I wanna sleep with you," she says in full voice.

"It's the middle of the night, darling. Go back to bed," I try, knowing it won't work. She's too stubborn, and I'm too tired to fight.

"I wanna sleep with you," she says, a hint of a whine in her voice. If I don't give in, she will definitely start wailing and wake everyone up.

*sigh*

"Fine," I say, lifting the sheets for the now smug Zoe to climb in. She wriggles about, getting comfortable, until I am wedged between her and my dead-to-the-world hubby. Just like that, she's out like a light, and I am stuck on my side, one arm pinned beneath me, the other flailing about in the cool air. My head is in the gap between our pillows, as she has claimed mine for herself.

# Frazzled

I close my eyes, attempting to go back to sleep. Not an easy feat when you have one arm slowly going numb underneath you. I try to wiggle into a better position, but there really is nowhere else to go.

When the clock reads 5:00 am, I give up. With moves like an Olympic gymnast, I manoeuvre myself out of bed without disturbing my sleeping angels and pull on my leggings and a singlet. I grab my running shoes and iPod and make my way out the door.

The air is cool but refreshing, giving me a new lease of life. I inhale deeply, emptying my mind. I set my stopwatch and take off.

I've never been much of a fitness junkie, but recently, I've found that running is a good way to clear my head, and it make me feel good too. The Universe seems to be against me this day though, as this happens:

I'm halfway through my run, when my body decides to betray me. Now, I don't know if it's a girl thing, or a 'me' thing, but my bodily functions have never been like clockwork. I never know when I'm going to need to… relieve myself.

Now I'm one-and-a-half km from home, and my body is going "*hey, so now that you're up and about, we need to evacuate the bowels. Now's good, right?*" I feel the twinge in my stomach at the same time as the pressure downstairs begins.

"No!" I scream inside my head. "You will not shit yourself!" I clench my butt-cheeks together (not easy when you are running), and will my legs to move faster (again, not so easy with clenched butt-cheeks).

# Frazzled

After what feels like forever, but I'm sure was only twenty seconds, the pressure subsides, and I am able to relax my sphincter. I run on for another thirty seconds before it comes back again.

This continues the entire one-and-a-half km back to my home. I'm glad that I didn't run into anyone, because I'm sure I was pulling some strange faces while trying to hold it in.

Once I reach the gate to my house, it's like my body just knows. The pressure builds as I sprint the last leg to the door and straight to the bathroom. Thank God it is empty!

I make it just in time.

Sweet release!

There is no better feeling! Well, that's not true, but you get what I mean.

Once finished, I wrestle with my sweat-soaked pants, inching them back up over my ample hips. I stumble out to the kitchen, sculling back half a bottle of water.

Zoe comes running out, arms outstretched. "Mummy!" she cries, happily flinging her arms around my sweaty, stinky body. Now *that's* love.

Of course, just to keep my head from getting too big, my oldest, Devon, decides to grace us with his presence at this time. He stomps through the kitchen, a scowl on his face when he sees me, grunting as he moves past.

*side note* *I think children get together and plan these mood swings of theirs, so that you can never*

# Frazzled

*relax. There are few times when all three of my children are happy to see me at any one time.*

I get to work preparing his lunch for school, wondering what I have done to annoy him this time. Probably something mundane. You know, like breathing. How dare I.

Teenagers are definitely put on this earth to test us. Just when you think you've got the hang of this parenting thing, they turn thirteen and throw you a curve ball. Suddenly everything you do is wrong. They start hanging out in their room more, and when you do actually see them out in the open, they are either rolling their eyes at you, or staring daggers. Something seems to make them hate you for no apparent reason, and then when you're about to have a breakdown over how much of a bad parent you must be, they flip the switch, and you catch a glimpse of that sweet kid you used to carry around on your hip. The one who loved you unconditionally.

In spite of this, I still want to try for that fourth child. I must be a sucker for punishment. Either that, or I'm seriously deranged. I'm leaning more towards the latter.

**Lunches** made and morning ritual of trying to get the girls dressed and ready, done. I grab my keys and tell them to get their drink bottle if they want it, and then go out to the car.

I unlock the doors for them, and they pile in. Devon sits in the front with his earphones in, not wanting to engage with his family. I strap the girls into their seats and run back to grab the grocery bags before pulling the door closed behind me.

I climb into the driver's seat and start the car.

"I wanted my drink bottle!" Zoe cries.

"I told you to get it if you wanted it. You had it in your hand before we went outside," I say.

"I don't have it! I want it!"

"Zoe, I told you to grab it. I'm not going back in. It's too late."

"But I want it!"

"Well, I'm sorry, but we're leaving, Devon needs to get to school," I say, putting the car in reverse and backing out of the drive. I'm already reaching the end of my tether after having to ask the girls ten times to put their shoes on.

"My seatbelt is too tight!" she yells.

"It's meant to be tight. That's what keeps you safe," I huff.

"It's too tight!" she yells again.

"It's not too tight. It's what it needs to be to keep you safe."

"I don't want to live with you anymore!" she screams. I wish I could say that this was the first time she has said this to me, but alas it is not. It has become her favourite thing to say when she doesn't get her way.

# Frazzled

Pushed to my limit, I'm ashamed to say I didn't handle it very well.

"Fine!" I yell back. "You find someone else to live with! They will strap you in just as tight as I do, because it's what parents do! They want their kids to be safe and not die if you have an accident!" By now, Devon has pulled his earphones out and is watching me with a mix of shock and amusement on his face.

"I want to live with someone else!" Zoe yells again.

"Well tough!" *I know, I have the best comebacks.* "You are stuck with me! And you will learn to respect what I say!"

Now, as soon as those words have left my mouth, the unmistakable sound of a minion's voice saying "Bottom" and then laughing, can be heard from my bag as I receive a text message. Devon looks at me and a giggle escapes his mouth. I'm still trying to be angry though, so I say "shut-up!" and then I too, break out in giggles. "Stop it!" I say, attempting to remain serious.

He just looks at me and says, "Bottom." Our eyes meet and we burst out laughing. Somehow, this went from being one of my most cringe-worthy moments of parenting, to one of my favourites. Any time that your teenager is laughing with you, instead of acting like you're someone they have to put up with, is a good time in my books.

I pull up outside his school and tell him I love him. He looks at me with a smirk, and I brace myself for a smartarse retort, but instead, he just says, "you too."

I smile. Maybe today won't be so bad.

# Frazzled

# Did Somebody Say Cheap?

**We** arrive at the supermarket and go through the list of rules again. "No running, no screaming, no arguing, no asking for things, keep your hands to yourself." The girls bob their heads up and down in agreement. I hoist them both into the trolley and give each of them a notepad—*learned my lesson from the last time.*

My new mission to try and save money in mind, I peruse the shelves, taking special care to work out what products offer us the best value. I find some reduced price meats that I can throw in the freezer until needed, no-name branded cereals for the children—because, let's face it, they'll never know the difference, no-name branded bulk tins of fruit, and even a bulk deal on toilet paper. So far, so good.

Ordinarily, I would buy a lot of the same things each week, not really taking the time to see what else there was on offer. It was quite an eye-opener. So many products I never knew existed! And the 'reduced to clear' baskets—what a gold mine!

As I continue scanning the shelves for bargains, I come across a do-it-yourself hair streaking kit. What a novel idea! I could do with a spruce up, and nothing

# Frazzled

makes you feel like a new woman, than a new haircut—or in my case, a freshening of colour.

I haven't been to a hairdresser in, oh… five or six years. Ever since we had to tighten the purse strings to accommodate the newest additions to our family. Before then, we (hubby and I) would both frequent the high-end salons and get all manner of treatments done. Alas that is no longer. Now I have a friend who cuts my hair, and I cut hubby's hair along with our kids. And before you ask, no I am not qualified, I just hack away until it looks passable.

I throw the kit into the trolley and carry on.

We make our way to the checkout, a smile brandished on my face as I feel seriously proud of myself for all my savvy budgeting. I start loading everything onto the conveyor belt, noting that it looks like I've bought more things than usual, but assuring myself it will be fine. I've bought lots of specials, remember.

The children have managed to keep themselves happy by pulling apart my notepads, so I decide to reward them with a lollipop each. I add that to the pile, along with a glossy magazine for me—I figure I deserve a treat after my hard work of child-wrangling and money-saving.

The cashier rings up my total and smiles pleasantly as she tells me what I owe. My jaw hits the floor. Apparently, I am not too good at saving money either. Somehow, in my misguided attempt at being frugal, I managed to purchase an extra $80 worth of stuff! How on Earth??

# Frazzled

Aghast, I pull out my card and surreptitiously sneak glances at my overflowing trolley, trying to find the culprit of this humongous overspend. Granted, I added hair dye and a magazine, but in the grand scheme of things, I saved us $100 by not going to the salon to have it done, so I don't count that.

There *is* a cheap bottle of wine and a box of beer for hubby, but we have children, and those things are a necessity. You try getting through the week without them.

I *did* purchase an unusual amount of toilet paper, but it was a great deal and I couldn't pass it up!

I *may* also have stocked up on bagels and cakes because they were reaching their best-before date and were reduced. I had plans of storing them in the freezer for when unexpected guests turn up. In hindsight, this was perhaps an unnecessary spend.

Okay. I get it. I'm not entrepreneurial or a budgeting goddess. Back to the drawing board me-thinks.

**Later** that evening, hubby and I are sitting on the couch watching television. The girls are tucked up in bed, and after about an hour of tag-team to-ing and fro-ing, we have managed to get them to settle. Devon has his best friend over, who happens to be the son of one

# Frazzled

of my best friends. He's like a second son to me—I've known him since he was a baby—so I don't think twice about pulling out the streaking kit while he's here.

I pull on the super-sexy plastic cap and secure it under my chin like one of those *Little House on the Prairie* type bonnets. I grab my crochet hook, and with a mirror perched on my lap, I slowly start pulling strands of hair through the cap. I'm about a third of the way through when I feel the presence of someone behind me. Thinking it's just one of the boys, I continue the painstakingly slow process.

A few minutes later, I see the outline of someone in my peripheral. They have been there for a while. I look up to see some random kid standing in my doorway, watching me. He lifts his hand and waves at me. "Hi," he says.

"Hi," I say back, too shocked to ask any questions.

Devon pokes his head out of his bedroom and says "Oh yeah, this is Phil."

I then realise this is the kid who lives next door to us, and they are apparently now friends.

I look back at my reflection in the mirror, noting the crazed look in my eyes and the wild hair poking through the holes in my tight plastic cap. Such a good look. If only I'd been given a heads up of our intended visitor, I may have freshened up somewhat. Not exactly the image I want to be remembered by.

There goes my "cool Mum" status. Oh well, at least the girls still think I'm cool. For now.

# The Seduction

**Surprisingly**, my home DIY streaking job does the trick quite well. It has certainly lightened my hair and given it a new lease of life. I wake with a bounce in my step, ready to face a new day—okay, so maybe I don't get out much, but a new hair cut can make you feel like a million bucks, you know.

Anyways, as I said, I'm feeling pretty good about myself right now. I climb into the shower and decide that perhaps tonight I might be up for a bit of 'late-night-action'. I grab the soap and begin lathering my legs ready to shave. Humming to myself, I drag the razor over my legs in long sweeps. On inspection, I can see there are *other* areas that could do with a trim as well. You know what I'm talking about.

When my husband and I first met, I used to get waxed on a regular basis. It was great! Now, I'm lucky if I get waxed once a year. Instead, I make do with a wet and dry razor. You know as well as I do, it's just not the same. It never gets to that silky smooth state, and let's face it, the hair grows back almost instantly.

Back then, I took pride in being somewhat of a sex goddess. And by sex goddess, I mean I was up for it at the drop of a hat, anytime, anywhere (ok, maybe not

# Frazzled

anywhere, but you get the picture). That gives me goddess status, right?

Of course, once kids came along, that had to be timed with their naps etc, but still, I was up for it.

Once child number three (bless her) came along, that all went out the window. It's not that I didn't want it, I just lacked the energy to do so. There's something so draining about being at the beck and call of three children and a husband. Every which way I turn, someone needs something from me. It can be exhausting.

So, I'm out of the shower now and the wet and dry has done a somewhat semi decent job. It may not be perfect, but it's the thought that counts. I'm sure hubby will be impressed with my efforts.

My preparations done; I go about the rest of my day with sexy thoughts running through my head. I contemplate sending hubby a sexy pic, to let him know what he's in for later, but that's really not all that easy to do. After about ten minutes of trying to get the best angles—where I don't have a double chin or muffin top—I give up.

The children have been watching a movie while I've been primping. Thank God for T.V! I notice the credits are rolling, so I switch it off and head for the kitchen to prepare a snack for them. Zoe is on my tail straight away.

"I want T.V."

"You've been watching it all morning. How about we do something outside?"

"I want T.V."

# Frazzled

"I know you do, but like I said, you've been watching it all morning. It's time to do something else."

"No. I was watching a movie. Movie is not T.V." she insists. I've got to give her credit for trying.

"You were watching the movie on the T.V. I've turned it off now, and it will stay off until later. Now, would you like a snack?"

Zoe sits on the floor, arms crossed stubbornly across her chest, brow pulled into a scowl. She turns her face away from me, making a "humph" sound. I can't help but grin at the cuteness.

"Okay, fine," I say, going to the cupboard. "I'm going to have a cookie. Would you like one, Ellie?" She bobs her head up and down enthusiastically. I hold the cookie jar out to her, letting her choose two. She proudly waves them in front of her sister's face.

"I got a cookie," she sings before taking a large bite.

"Humph!" Zoe says again, though I can see her looking out of the corner of her eyes at the jar in my hand.

"Would you like one, Zoe?" I ask again, shaking the jar. "They're really good," I sing.

"I want T.V." she mutters, shuffling her little body along the floor until she is in front of me. She looks up at me, scowl still in place. Slowly, her forehead smooths out and her eyes soften. Her hand darts out and she snaffles two cookies in her hand, grinning from ear to ear. I put the cookie jar away and scoop her into my arms, planting a kiss on her nose. She puckers up her

# Frazzled

cookie-crumbed lips and returns the favour before whispering in my ear. "I want T.V."

**I** spend the majority of the day breaking up arguments between the two girls. They can't seem to agree on anything today. They want to play with the same toys at the same time, but not together. One wants to draw, while the other wants to play on the see-saw.

I manage to wrangle them into some sort of an order by the time hubby comes home. Dinner is on the table, and the house is not quite the bombsite it had been. There is baking in the cupboard for lunches tomorrow, and the washing in the basket is clean and folded. I'm starting to feel rather tired, but I made plans to seduce my husband, and I have every intention of sticking to the plan.

Bedtime arrives, and thankfully, the children go straight to sleep. Hubby goes to have a shower, and I decide to get ready in the bedroom.

I strip down and apply some moisturiser to my legs, making them feel even smoother. I slip into my satin nightie—noting that it feels a smidge tighter than I remember it being. I pull back the sheets and slide in, patiently waiting for his return.

It's a little chilly, so I snuggle deeper under the blankets to warm up. I can feel the weight of the day

# Frazzled

pressing on my eyelids, so decide to 'rest' my eyes, telling myself that I'll hear him come into the room.

Three o'clock, and I wake up with drool on my chin, hubby peacefully snoring beside me. Oh well. There's always tomorrow.

# Seriously?

**Thud**, thud, thud, thud…

I roll over, holding the sheet open for Zoe to climb into bed for our morning cuddles while hubby gets ready for work. She clambers in, making herself comfortable. Instead of her usual babble, she snuggles up against me, smelly giraffe grasped firmly in her hands, and drifts back to sleep. It's one of those adorable moments when you really appreciate having children.

I shift positions so I'm lying on my back. Zoe wakes, rolls towards me and links her arm through mine.

"I'm the only child who loves you," she whispers.

*Um, what now?*

"What?" I ask, unsure whether I should be creeped out or flattered.

"I'm the only child who loves you," she says again. Definitely no mistaking it.

"Uh, what about Ellie and Devon?" I ask. "I'm pretty sure they love me too."

"No. Just me," she says matter-of-factly. "Is it breakfast time?"

# Frazzled

"I… uh…" I stutter, trying to find my words as I deal with the sudden change of topic. "Yeah, sure. Go see Daddy, I'll be up in a minute."

I throw my arm across my face, groaning. I really don't feel like adulting today. Even with my relatively restful sleep, I still feel exhausted.

I clamber out of bed, pulling on my fluffy bathrobe and pink bunny slippers and shuffle out to the kitchen.

"Morning," hubby says, planting a kiss on my forehead.

"Morning," I say back. "D'you know what your daughter said to me this morning?" I ask. He stares blankly, his shoulder lifting slightly in a shrug. "She said that she's the only child that loves me. I don't even know how to take that."

He pours a cup of tea and hands it to me. "Maybe it's just her way of saying that she *really* loves you. Like, more than anyone else does." He shrugs again. "I dunno."

"I guess. She *has* taken to chanting "I love you, I love you, I love you the MOST!" when we are in stores."

"There you go, she just *really obsessively* loves you." He grins, pulling me in for a hug before he heads out the door.

I carry my tea into the lounge and sit on the couch. Ellie creeps out of her room, rubbing her eyes. She gives me a sleepy smile before heading for the bathroom. They're so adorable when they've just woken up. Well… sometimes.

# Frazzled

I'm staring off into space when Ellie comes back into my line of sight. She has her head in the fridge, probably getting the milk for her cereal. I look over to Zoe, who is sitting at the table, her legs swinging beneath her as she eats her breakfast. I give her a smile and turn my attention back to the kitchen. Ellie is still in the fridge.

"What are you doing?" I ask.

"Nothing," she replies, quickly closing the fridge. She runs up to me, climbing onto my lap. I note the milk moustache across her top lip.

"Were you pouring a glass of milk?" I ask.

"No," she says, shaking her head with a grin.

"Are you sure? I can see milk on your face."

"No, I didn't," she says adamantly.

I look at her sceptically. She clearly has milk on her face. I lift her onto the couch and go to the fridge to investigate. I open the door to see a puddle of milk trailing underneath.

"Ellie, are you sure you didn't take some milk?" I ask again, giving her one more chance to come clean.

"No, I didn't." She shakes her head firmly.

"There's milk on the floor and milk on your face. Please tell me you didn't drink from the bottle." I stare at her, waiting.

"Yes," she whispers. "I did." Her lips curl downwards, and she looks at the floor.

"Ellie! That's how germs are spread. Now no one else can drink the milk. I'm very disappointed that you did that, *and* that you lied about it." I fold my arms across my chest.

# Frazzled

"I'm sorry," she whispers. "I just really wanted a drink of milk."

"Why didn't you get a glass then?"

She shrugs her shoulders. I sigh. At least I was able to get my morning cup of tea beforehand.

**I'm** still working up the courage to tell hubby that I want another baby. I was kind of hoping I would have made some progress on my plan by now. I mean, I'm not getting any younger.

Money making, and money saving don't appear to be my strong suits, so I may as well work on getting Zoe out of our room at night. It's not like I haven't tried. It's just that when she stumbles in in the middle of the night, I'm quite often half asleep and don't even realise that she's in there until I wake up an hour or so later, when I'm overheating from the extra body sandwiching me in. The other times, I assume that it's almost time to get up, and so I invite her in for a cuddle, only to realise (again an hour or so later) that it was actually only midnight when she came in, and not 5:00 am as I first thought.

Enough is enough. No more Mrs Nice Mum. From now on, I will pick her up and put her back in her own bed. No excuses. I will implement the plan at bedtime.

# Frazzled

**When** six o'clock rolls around, I send the girls to change into their pyjamas and brush their teeth. I gather up their discarded clothes and carry them to the laundry, tidying things as I go. I meet them back at the couch, both eagerly waiting with a story in hand.

"Before we read our bedtime story, we need to go over a new rule, okay?" I smile reassuringly. "The new rule is, we always sleep ALL night, in our OWN bed." I read somewhere that you should reinforce rules with positive language and not focus on what they shouldn't do but on what they should. I'm willing to try anything at this point. "Alright? Say it with me!" I say enthusiastically. "We always sleep ALL night, in our OWN bed," we say together.

Satisfied that they understand, I sit back and read their bedtime stories. They kiss us goodnight and then scramble to their beds. We each go in to tuck them in and before I leave, I repeat the rule again.

"All night...own bed!" Zoe joins in heartily. I may be onto something here! I head back out to the lounge to join hubby. He looks at me with a raised brow.

"All night, own bed?" he asks.

"It's the new rule." I smile. "I'm trying to get Zoe to stay in her own bed so we can, ya know, *get busy* without having to worry about being interrupted." I make some crude motions with my pelvis.

# Frazzled

"So, what I'm hearing is, I'm getting lucky tonight?" he probes, a grin playing across his face. I can't help but giggle.

"Easy there, Tiger. We have to see if it actually works first."

"So, you're saying there's a chance I'm getting lucky tonight?" he asks, winking at me suggestively.

I slap his shoulder playfully. "We'll see." I settle in beside him, ready to watch the movie we've been waiting to see.

Half an hour in and Ellie comes out carrying a pair of knickers and smirking.

"What are you doing?" I ask.

"I had an accident," she says, trying to conceal her complacent smile.

"You had better be joking," I say. "It's not an accident if you are still awake, Ellie." I sigh and go into the bedroom to strip the sheets off her bed. The blanket on top has a wet patch, but it doesn't appear to have gone all the way through the bedding. I gather the blanket into a bundle and make my way out to the laundry, passing Ellie on the way. "The sheets aren't wet, so you can just sleep on top of those," I say. She nods and mopes into the bedroom.

I go back in to see her. "Why did you do that, Ellie?" I ask.

She looks me in the eye and says, "Because I thought it would go all the way through, and I wanted to sleep on the floor."

# Frazzled

My mouth gapes open. "Are you serious right now? You peed in your bed so that you could sleep on the floor?!"

"Yeah." She nods solemnly.

"Why didn't you just get on the floor and go to sleep?!"

"I didn't think I would be allowed to," she says.

Kid logic. I shake my head in disbelief and walk out the door, lost for words.

"Did you hear that?" I ask hubby, hitching my thumb over my shoulder towards the bedroom. "She did it on purpose, so that she could sleep on the floor!" I say incredulously. I don't know whether to laugh or cry.

"Thinking outside the square, I guess," hubby says, shrugging his shoulders, trying to conceal his grin. I glare at him. He sighs. "I'm not getting lucky now, am I?"

# And it Continues

**After** throwing the blanket into the washing machine, I wash my hands three times, scrubbing with a brush to make sure there is no pee still left on my hands. I stomp into the kitchen and make myself a coffee, then head straight for the bedroom. I don't even care about the movie anymore.

I peel off my clothes, leaving them in a heap on the floor to be dealt with tomorrow. My flannel pyjamas sit by my pillow, begging me to wear them. I pull them on and instantly feel warm and snug. I climb into bed and grab my book from the dresser. It's early, but I'm still wound up about Ellie's incident, and reading is the one thing I can count on to take my mind off it.

*"Maddi stared at her reflection as she tried to mentally psych herself up for her first ever teaching gig..."*

*I* need to mentally psych myself up for dealing with these children!

Who pees on a bed deliberately??

Who does that?

I silently berate myself for letting this get to me and ruin my reading time. Reading is my favourite pastime and I will *not* let this silly event spoil it for me.

# Frazzled

I take a swig of my coffee and snuggle further into my blankets, pulling them up around my ears, so only my hands and head are exposed. Not the easiest position for reading, but you learn to adapt. The trick is to not fall asleep while still reading. That will only end in pain as the book falls on your face. Believe me, I've done it.

My mind attempts to wander a few more times, but it isn't long before the story captivates me, and my tensions slowly drift away. In fact, I can actually see the funny side to this. At least I'll have a story to tell people!

Hubby slinks into the bedroom and cautiously lies down on top of the blankets. He eyes me warily. "So... you still mad at me?" he asks.

I glance up from my pages. "No." I let out a long breath. "I wasn't really mad at you." Closing my book, I turn to face him. "I just feel like I spend all my time cleaning up after people. I can't believe she would do something like that deliberately."

"Yeah, it was pretty deviant. She must take after you." He grins, wiggling his eyebrows at me.

I swipe my book at his shoulder. "Hey!" I say, feigning shock. My face betrays me though and I find myself giggling with him. It feels good to laugh about it.

"So..." He walks his fingers up my arm, a mischievous grin playing across his face as he winks at me. "You wanna *get busy?*" He mimics my earlier pelvic thrusting motions, causing me to giggle even more. He wraps his arm around me, pulling me against

# Frazzled

him as he continues to thrust his hips at me through the blankets. He buries his head in the crook of my neck, kissing up towards my ear—something he knows sends me into fits of hysterics.

"Stop!" I pant breathlessly. "I'll pee my pants!" I squeal as I wriggle in an attempt to free myself from his embrace.

"Now, now. There'll be no more wet beds in this house tonight!" he teases.

I finally manage to pull myself away and dart out of bed, running for the bathroom. Having three children will do that to you. I dread the day I actually *do* pee my pants.

Anywho, I finish up and head back to the bedroom. Hubby has somehow managed to light a selection of candles and placed them around the room, as well as stripping himself starkers.

*How long was I in there?*

He's standing there, hands on hips, looking super proud of himself. How can I turn that down?

I wrap my arms around his waist and standing on tiptoes, I kiss him. "Thank you," I whisper.

**Content** and relaxed, we fall asleep in each other's arms. He on his back, and me curled up to his side, his arm draped around my shoulders. My leg is flung over

# Frazzled

his keeping him close. My days are spent so busy with children all over me, that I sometimes forget how nice it is to snuggle up to the warm body of my husband.

At some point during the night, I roll onto my stomach, my leg still entwined with hubby's, but the rest of me has moved away, seeking the coolness of the empty space beside me.

I vaguely notice that the blankets feel quite heavy on me, and I try to shrug them off, but they won't budge. I turn to see Zoe, peacefully sleeping on my back. I wiggle and whisper, "Zoe, you need to go back to your bed now, sweetheart."

I'm so exhausted that I fall back to sleep without even making sure she has listened to me.

"Zoe, get up. Go and put your knickers in the laundry."

*What?*

I suddenly feel the wetness seeping through the blanket. My eyes blink open. "What's going on?" I mumble.

"Zoe has wet the bed," hubby says.

"*Our* bed?" I ask, hoping that I had imagined the wetness and that it was, in fact, her own bed that she had wet.

"Yeah, our bed. The mother of all pees." He switches the light on, and I see what he's talking about. There is a wet patch taking up about a third of our blanket!

"Aww, Zoe!" I groan.

She looks up at me with her big brown eyes, tears glistening. "I'm sorry, Mummy," she stutters, sniffing.

# Frazzled

"Come on, let's get you cleaned up." I take her hand and lead her to the bathroom to wash her and change her clothes, while hubby takes all the blankets off our bed and throws them into the laundry.

"Which couch d'you want?" he asks me.

I look at his six-foot frame and shrug. "You take the couch; I'll sleep on a bean bag." I put Zoe back into her own bed and kiss her cheek. "Please try to sleep the rest of the night in your own bed, okay?" She nods, gripping giraffe in her pudgy little hands.

I grab my pillow and drag a bean bag out into the middle of the lounge floor. I curl into a ball and endeavour to get back to sleep. Hubby switches off the light, and then I feel him gently place a blanket over me before he goes to his couch.

I love that man.

# Just When You Thought It Was Safe

I should have known.

We had one glorious week without any mishaps. No wet beds, no nightly visitors, no milk bandits.

It was bound to happen, of course. We got too comfortable.

It's so easy to let your guard down when things finally start going right. Take my word for it, you should Never. Ever. Let your guard down. Not when you have tiny people in your midst. They know just when to reign it in and be all cute as pie, and then Bam! They throw you something you aren't prepared for.

We already had a busy weekend planned. Not only did we have to repaint the girls' bedroom (let's just say, someone likes to draw and doesn't care what the canvas is), but hubby also had plenty of work in the garden to attend to before his parents visited, and I was trying my luck at yet another job I could do from home. The only thing is, I needed some peace and quiet to do it. I told everyone I needed an hour to get some work done, and then I shut myself in the bedroom.

That was my mistake right there. I should never have trusted them to behave without my watchful eye.

# Frazzled

Devon would usually look after them for me in times such as these, but he had stayed at a friend's house the night before and wasn't due back just yet.

So anyways, the hour goes by and I'm still perched on my bed, scrolling through documents on the laptop to make sure I hadn't missed anything, when Devon arrives home and knocks on the door.

"Ah, you're not going to be happy," he says.

"What's happened?" I ask, still staring at the screen.

"There's hair all over the floor," he says, waving my scissors at me.

"What?!"

"I think they've cut some of their toys' hair too."

"Oh God! Ellie! Zoe! Here, now!" I holler, closing the laptop and pushing it aside.

*Why had I shut the door?*

*Why had I not been paying more attention?*

*How much damage was done?*

The girls come running in, both ready with excuses.

"It was Ellie, she did it," Zoe says, grinning. One half of her hair still looks normal, but I can see several large chunks taken from around the front on the other side.

"Zoe did it too!" Ellie throws in there. "She stole them!"

"No! Ellie did!" Zoe argues.

"I don't care who took them, you both know you're not allowed to play with scissors. You both know that that was naughty, and you still did it

# Frazzled

anyway." I run my hand through my own hair and summon them to me. "Let me have a look at you."

Ellie's hair has only a few pieces missing, confirming my suspicions that she was the instigator. On closer inspection, I see that Zoe has had more cut off than I first thought. There is a big chunk cut from the back, halfway up her head, and more around the side. I let out a long sigh.

"You understand how dangerous this was, don't you? You could have cut yourselves." I pause, plucking a clump of Zoe's hair in between my thumb and finger. "I'm going to have to try and fix this. I'm very disappointed in you girls."

"It was Ellie!" Zoe pouts at me, her eyes filling with tears.

"Honey, I know Ellie cut your hair, but you let her do it. You should have come and told Mummy that she had the scissors," I explain, holding her squishy cheeks in my hands.

*I'm not ready to cut my baby's hair short. She's not going to look like a baby anymore.*

I kiss her forehead, willing myself not to cry over something so trivial. I lead her out to the lounge and sit her down on a stool while I brace myself for what I'm about to do.

I take a deep breath, and then, taking a large handful of her hair, I begin to snip. I cut it as straight as I can, but there are still some shorter pieces up the back that I can't get to blend in. I'm not exactly trained in this stuff. Knowing our money situation though, I don't have much of a choice.

# Frazzled

No matter how hard I try, I cannot get it even. Closing my eyes, I think back to what I had seen my friend do to blend. I hold my fingers on an angle, mimicking her actions and snip.

Nope. That was most certainly not the right thing to do.

Every time I adjust one side, the other side appears longer, so I snip some more. At this rate, I am going to have to shave it off! Cutting girls' hair is a lot harder than men's!

I do the only thing I can. I send an SOS text to my friend. I really don't want to interrupt her weekend, but hubby's parents are going to be visiting any minute, and I really don't want them to see the mess I've made of our daughter's hair!

Being the true friend that she is, she drops everything and comes to my rescue. Zoe's hair is now short in the back, gradually getting longer towards the front. She even managed to blend in the super short piece that I had cut accidentally. In the nick of time too, I might add. As she heads out the door, the in-laws pull up the drive. Phew!

*Side note: Zoe looks pretty darn cute with her new pixie cut (not that I can admit that to them—don't want them getting any more ideas!).*

### Frazzled

# Money, Money, Money

**The** in-laws have left, and I'm in the kitchen preparing dinner. Ellie runs past me in a rush to get to the bathroom. I tut and shake my head. I've told them time and time again not to wait until they are busting for the loo, but will they listen?

I hear the unmistakeable sound of the toilet seat being smacked against the bowl as she does the 'toilet dance' while trying to wriggle her pants off. The pounding of her feet stops, and I pause, listening.

"Ellie? Did you make it?" I call out, holding my breath.

"Yes!" she calls out before starting off on a warbled rendition of *Twinkle Twinkle Little Star*. I guess the acoustics in there are pretty good because this is a regular thing for her. If I didn't tell her to get out, I think she would sit there for hours, singing away.

This time though, I leave her there. It's nice to hear her sounding so happy, and it's relaxing to listen to while I cut veggies.

I finish slicing and dicing and throw the veggies into the large saucepan simmering on the stove. Grabbing a teaspoon, I give it a quick taste test.

"Hmm, a bit more salt and pepper," I say to myself as I season the soup. I go to the cupboard and pull out

# Frazzled

some lentils and barley and throw those in too. "Perfect!" Reducing the heat so it will continue to just blip away for a few hours, I realise Ellie is still in the bathroom. What's more, the singing has ceased. This normally only means one thing.

She is up to mischief.

"Ellie? Honey, what are you doing?" I ask, wiping my hands on a tea towel as I make my way to the bathroom.

"Nothing!" she calls out, but I can hear her scurrying about. I push the door open, and she is standing at the sink with a guilty look on her face.

"What have you been up to?" I ask, noting the plastic jug in her hand and the open tube of toothpaste on the vanity.

"Nothing," she whispers, her big hazel eyes peering up at me. I look inside the jug and see that the bottom is coated with toothpaste. I turn back to her, a questioning look in my eyes. "I was making a mixture," she admits, dropping her gaze.

I can see the remnants of more toothpaste in the sink where she has attempted to dispose of her little concoction.

"What were you mixing it with?" I ask.

"Water," she says, though her eyes dart to the floor in the middle of the room, betraying her. I turn to see what has her attention and discover the liquid soap dispenser is lying on the floor, empty. "And some soap," she whispers.

"Ellie, this was full! I only just filled it up yesterday."

# Frazzled

"Sorry, Mummy. I just wanted to make a mixture," she says again, scuffing her toe along the floor.

"A mixture for what?" I demand.

"Just a mixture," she says.

I get down to her level. "Ellie, these things cost money. You can't just waste them like that. What are we supposed to wash our hands with now?"

She beams at me. "We can use water, Mummy."

"Yes, we can. But you need the soap to get rid of the germs. We don't want to spread germs, do we?"

"No, Mummy." She shakes her head, her chocolate-brown curls bobbing around her face.

"We'll need to buy some more soap now, won't we? You're not going to do that again, are you?" I ask, holding her hands in mine.

"No, Mummy. I'm sorry," she says, throwing her arms around my neck and giving me a big cuddle.

"It's okay, sweetheart. Money is just a bit tight, so we can't be wasting things, okay?"

"Okay," she says, her voice muffled against my shoulder. She pulls away and looks at me with the sweetest expression. "I could pay for it with my pocket money," she says. I feel my eyes start to well up, both at the gesture, and at the fact that it even has to come to this. I don't want my kids to feel like they have to pay for things. Especially not essential items like soap. I silently chastise myself for mentioning money at all.

I shake my head. "Thank you, sweetheart, but you don't have to do that. Mummy and Daddy will buy the soap." I place a kiss on her nose, and she grins at me before bouncing off to her room to play.

# Frazzled

I traipse back to the kitchen and stir the soup listlessly. My mind drifts off, and I can't stop thinking about the fact that my four-year-old thinks she needs to pay for household things.

Did I do the right thing by telling her that we can't afford to waste things? I *do* want my children to have a better grasp on the value of money than I did. The amount of money I wasted on frivolous things when I was younger… if only I had saved more, we wouldn't be in such a tight position now. I don't want my kids to end up struggling the way we do, but is four too young to begin that?

Hubby sneaks up behind me and slips his hands around my waist, pulling me against him. He kisses my neck.

"Mmmm, smells good," he says, eyeing the soup.

"Mmhmm," I say.

"Everything okay?" he asks, planting another kiss on my neck, giving me goosebumps.

"Yeah," I sigh. "I just caught Ellie mixing the liquid soap and toothpaste in the bathroom. I told her we couldn't afford to waste it and she offered to pay for a new one. I feel bad now."

"Are you kidding? You're teaching our daughter how the world works. You have no reason to feel bad." He takes the spoon from my hand, setting it on the counter and turning me to face him. "You're a great Mum. Don't be so hard on yourself."

I smile up at him. How did I get to be so lucky?

# III Feelings

**I** wake the next morning with a terrible headache. Zoe had been in and out of our room all night, and is currently curled into my back, snoring her little head off. I roll over, pulling her into my arms for a cuddle. Something about her squishy little arms and hands wrapped around my neck always makes me feel better. Even though it was a shitty night's sleep, I can't help but smile.

She snuggles in further, holding me tightly. I kiss her forehead and close my eyes again, breathing in the scent of her shampoo. I wish it could always be like this. Cuddles and kisses.

Of course, hubby has to go to work, so his alarm goes off, calling an end to the peacefulness. Zoe's eyes peep open, and she says, very loudly of course, "Good morning!"

No matter how little sleep she has had, she is always so chipper in the mornings. Don't get me wrong, I am definitely a morning person myself, but I still need my eight hours to be able to function.

"Can I have T.V?" Zoe asks, grinning up at me.

"Sorry, sweetheart, not today. We have an appointment this morning. We don't want to be late."

# Frazzled

"But… but you never let me watch T.V!" she cries, turning away from me as she huffs and puffs.

"Honey, I'm not saying you can't watch T.V. at all, I'm just saying, not this morning. You can watch it when we get back," I say, knowing full well that this is not going to go down with her.

"But I want it now!" she demands, scrunching her hands into fists around her smelly giraffe.

*Deep breaths. In through the nose and out through the mouth.*

"I know you do, but like I said, we have an appointment and we can't be late."

"We won't be late if I watch T.V," she mumbles.

I have to laugh at that. "Zoe, you get distracted by T.V. You can watch it when we get home."

"I'm not going!"

"Fine. You won't get T.V. at all then." I throw the blanket off me and stalk out to the kitchen.

"At it already, huh?" hubby asks as I storm past him.

"She's so stubborn!" I say, throwing my hands in the air as I continue through to the bathroom.

"I wonder where she gets that from," he says, averting his eyes as he sips his coffee, a smile playing on his lips.

"I…you…" I stutter, pointing my finger at him. He puts his cup down, grinning at me.

"Come here," he says, walking over to me and wrapping me in his arms.

"I'm not stubborn," I mutter against his chest.

"No, not at all, my love."

# Frazzled

**After** a shower and some coffee, I'm feeling somewhat prepared for the day ahead. I decide that a trip to the park is in order. Nothing like a bit of fresh air to make you really appreciate being alive.

I make sure the girls are suitably clothed—jackets and gloves—for the cool autumn weather. It takes several arguments about the appropriateness of jandals in this temperature, but I eventually get them strapped in the car—gumboots and all. I send a quick text to my friend, asking her to meet us at the park, and then we hit the road.

Due to the freshness of the wind, I find a park right in front of the playground. The girls clamber out of the car and run for the swings while I grab a bag with spare clothes and snacks—you learn early on in motherhood that snacks are a necessity to have. I can't tell you the number of times that we would visit someone, and the first thing said is, "I'm hungry". As if you never feed your children. That and "I need the toilet". Apparently other people's toilets are a novelty. Don't ask me why.

*Did I tell you about the time we were visiting a friend and Zoe didn't quite make it in time? That was a whole lot of mess I was not impressed to find. Who picks faecal matter up with their bare hands and proceeds to smear it on the wall and toilet seat?*

*My daughter, that's who.*

Anyways, I hoist the bag onto my shoulder and follow them to the swings. Ellie is jumping on the spot while holding the chain rope in an attempt to lift herself up. I've got to give her credit for trying. I lift her up

# Frazzled

and give her a gentle push, reminding her that she needs to swing her legs to keep it moving.

I fumble about trying to get Zoe's legs into the individual leg holes of the baby swing—there really should be a better way of doing this. I stuff giraffe down the front for some extra padding and proceed to push her until she is squealing with laughter. You have to time it just right. If you push too far, then it stops being fun and their whole face turns from joy to terror in a matter of seconds.

I watch them giggling away, their cheeks pink from the fresh air, their breaths puffing out visibly. These moments are ones I cherish. I love the sound of their laughter. It makes my heart happy.

A familiar car pulls up beside mine, and I wave as Carla climbs out of the car with her daughter in tow.

Carla is one of my oldest friends. We met twelve years ago, when our first children were babies. Both new mothers, we'd sought each other out by way of a column in one of those women's magazines. She posted an ad asking for a penpal, and I answered. We've been friends ever since.

Like me, Carla has a teenager, as well as a soon-to-be school kid. Somehow, we managed to time our pregnancies close to each other. We're like pregnancy sisters or something.

"Hey!" she calls out as she traipses through the fallen leaves. "How's it going?"

"Pretty good, you?" I ask, throwing my arms around her and giving a squeeze.

# Frazzled

"Yeah, the same. It feels like ages since we caught up last."

"I know. We really should make more time for each other." I grin. We have this exact same conversation every time we get together. "So, the baby business is still out of action?" I ask as we walk to one of the nearby seats.

"Yeah. I tried to convince him we needed another, but ya know, he wants a house," she says with a hint of sarcasm in her voice.

"I get that, I guess." I look down at my hands in my lap, then back to the children.

"Oh no. I know that look. What's up?"

"No, nothing. I mean…" I try to smile, though I can feel tears brimming. Something about being around friends does that to me. "I want another one," I whisper with a wince.

Carla snorts out a laugh. "Are you serious?" She looks at me and must notice the tears. "Oh God, you are serious, aren't you?"

I just nod.

"I take it he doesn't want to?" she probes.

"I don't even know! I'm too chicken to bring it up." I laugh at my ridiculousness. "Isn't that stupid?"

"What're you going to do? Surprise baby?" she asks, nudging her elbow into my arm with a grin. She always knows what to say.

"God, could you imagine?" I pause, trying to decide if I should tell her or not. "I actually thought I was a few months ago. False alarm though."

"Is that what made you change your mind?"

# Frazzled

"Yeah. I thought I was okay with not having any more until I thought I was going to have another one, and now I can't get it out of my head."

"You don't think it'll pass?"

"I don't know. Maybe." *No.*

We sit in silence, watching the children as their swings slow. Zoe flaps her arms about, trying to get my attention.

"I better go get her down," I say, walking towards them. "Why don't you guys go and play in the sandpit?" I say when I reach them.

"What a good idea. Go and play for ten minutes, and then we can have a snack."

The children run off, Zoe lagging behind. We meander back to our seat.

"You know, I don't think he'll react that badly," she says. "He's great with the kids, and he really loves you. That man would do anything for you. I think he'll surprise you."

"I know. I don't know why I'm being so silly."

"Just talk to him. The worst that can happen is he says no."

"You're right. I know you are. I'll do it. I just have to find the right moment."

"Well don't take too long." She looks me up and down. "You're not getting any younger, and the old biological clock won't tick for much longer." She pokes her tongue between her teeth, waggling her brows.

*She'll keep.*

# Out Like a Light

**Thud**, thud, thud…

I peel my eyes open and see the silhouette of Zoe standing beside the bed. Without a word, I pull the sheet back in anticipation of her climbing in.

"I don't want to get into bed with you," she says in her 'outside voice'—you know, in case I wasn't awake already. "I need a drink and I can't find my drink bottle."

"It's on the windowsill," I mumble, my face smooshed into the pillow still.

"I don't want that one. I want the other one."

"Well, I don't know where it is. Go and see if it's on the bench."

She scampers off, and I hear her stumbling about in the kitchen. "It's not here!" she yells.

"It's probably been put away then," I call back in frustration. If anyone hadn't woken already, I'm sure they will have by now.

I hear cupboards being opened and slammed shut. She rummages through the plastic containers without a care for how much noise she's making. "It's not here!" she yells again.

I sigh, throwing the sheets off me and clambering out to her.

# Frazzled

"Go and get the other one then. I'll fill it with fresh water."

I rub my eyes and squint at the clock on the microwave. Two-thirty-six! No wonder I'm still half asleep.

I fill her bottle and send her on her way.

Not even five minutes later, my ears prick up to the sound of more footsteps. This time it's Ellie. "I just want a quick cuddle," she says, already climbing in beside me. She rarely does this, so I take advantage of the moment and wrap my arms around her. We both fall back to sleep.

About an hour later, I'm woken once again as I feel Ellie begin to roll over towards the edge of the bed. Thinking she's getting up to go back to her own bed, I release her from my grip, only to find that she tumbles to the floor.

"Are you okay?" I ask, leaning down to look at her.

"I'm fine," she replies, getting to her feet and brushing herself off. "It was just a little bump." She climbs back into bed and threads her arms around my neck.

"You're a silly muffin," I say, planting a kiss on her forehead.

"I love you, Mummy," she says.

"I love you too."

"I love you more," she whispers.

"Nope, not possible. I love you mostest."

She giggles. "No, I love you one thousand and six thousand and twenty-one!"

# Frazzled

"Wow, that much? You know what? I still love you even more than that," I say, kissing her again. "Now go back to sleep."

"Okay, Mummy." She snuggles in and as I'm drifting back to sleep, I hear the faintest voice whisper, "I love you more."

# Sugar and Spice

**Another** week rolls by and I still haven't plucked up the nerve to have 'the conversation' with hubby. I don't even know how to broach the subject to be honest. We had made our decision, together. A decision that I was happy with, at the time. I mean, I was sleep deprived (that still hasn't changed), and money was tight (also hasn't changed), and I was struggling with my emotions (okay so maybe everything is still the same). I was stressed out.

Yes, I know I am still all of the above, but the thought of shutting up shop for good… that just doesn't sit right with me. It makes me feel sad to think that there will be no more babies. If I had known when I was pregnant with Zoe that she would be the last, I would have savoured it more. Instead, I was in a hurry for her to come out.

Okay, so maybe I was humongous and uncomfortable. And maybe I was over it. But I'm sure, had I known, I would've felt differently. I mean, I thought I still had more time.

I know hubby was just trying to ease my stress. He hates it when I get emotional. I'm a crier. I cry when I'm sad, I cry when I'm happy, hell, I even cry when I'm hungry! It can be a lot for a guy to take on, and I

# Frazzled

know that deep down, he was just trying to keep me happy by suggesting that we stop. And I thought I was okay with it. I really did.

Now, every time I see a new-born baby, or a lady with a beautiful baby bump, I feel an emptiness inside. My babies aren't babies anymore. They're growing bigger every day, and it's only a matter of time before they are off to school. Not to mention my eldest will be thinking about Uni soon. He'll be moving in less than five years, and that scares me. I want so much to hold on to them and keep them safe in my arms forever. I'm not ready for them to be out in the world without me.

Is that selfish? To want another baby because I'm not ready to let go? It probably is. I can't help the way my heart feels though. I can only hope that hubby will understand.

I spend the morning baking a coffee cake with buttercream icing. I get the girls to help me decorate it with chocolate drops and sprinkles before setting it in the centre of the table. It's hubby's favourite, and I'm not afraid to use anything at my disposal to help convince him we should do this.

A roast chicken waits in the oven, and for once, the house is actually looking rather tidy. I may have bribed the girls with a movie, but that's beside the point.

# Frazzled

When hubby walks in, I bustle about the kitchen, whisking up homemade gravy to go over the veggies. He slips his arms around my waist and snuggles into my back.

"Dinner smells great! What's the occasion?" he asks.

"No occasion. I just wanted to treat you. You work so hard all week." I feel his smile against my neck and know that he suspects something is up.

"Mmmhmmm," he says, spinning me to face him with a smirk on his face. "What have you done?"

I crinkle my brow, trying to pull off the puzzled look. "Whatever do you mean?" I ask, playing dumb.

He laughs, kissing my forehead. "Something's up." He motions to the cake and pristine kitchen. "I can tell."

"Nope. I just love you," I say sweetly, kissing his nose. "Now, go wash up for dinner." He shakes his head, chuckling to himself as he ushers the children into the bathroom with him.

"Come on, kids, let's go wash up."

I turn back to the gravy, which has thickened up nicely. I pour it into the gravy boat and carry it out to the table. I finish loading the plates with chicken and veggies and hand them to everyone as they come back through.

We all take our seats, and Ellie starts off our usual dinner conversation.

"What was your favourite part of the day, Mum?" she asks, stuffing a forkful of food into her mouth.

# Frazzled

"Hmmm, I think it was our cuddles this morning," I say, smiling at her.

"What was your favourite part of the day, Dad?" Zoe pipes up.

"Coming home to this lovely cooked meal," he says, meeting my eyes with a look of pure pleasure. And just like that, I realise I have no need to be so worried. This man loves me. If I'm completely honest, I know that he tries his best every day to make sure I'm happy and our kids have everything they need. That's all he's ever wanted. My happiness.

But what does *he* want? That's the real question.

I watch him talking and laughing with our children. I see the sparkle in his eyes as he listens intently to their stories about their day. I notice the little private jokes he and Devon share.

He is such a great Dad. Something I think surprised him. He never wanted children until he met me. As I've said before, becoming a mother was the only thing I was sure of in my life. It was a deal-breaker for me, and I guess he saw me as worth it because here we are, three children later, and still very much in love.

I know he will do whatever he can to continue to keep me happy, and I will do the same for him. Whether these two ideas are one and the same is another thing. I still want another baby, but watching him interact with the children we already have; I know I will be okay if it turns out he doesn't want any more. He will help me fill the void once our children have moved on and no longer need me as much.

# Frazzled

My heart stops hammering in my chest and I can relax and enjoy the company of the family I love so dearly. For all our ups and downs, I know I'm lucky to be a part of something so special, and for that, I am grateful.

# Full Circle

**We** never did have that conversation.

No. I just realised that I already had the perfect little family unit. If it's not broken, don't fix it, right?

I stopped stressing about money and put all my energy into enjoying my children while they're still young and willing to give me their unconditional love. I savour those stolen moments, those middle-of-the-night cuddles, those warbled songs from the bathroom.

I am so rocking this in-the-moment parenting that I don't even notice I still haven't had my period. Not since before the dreaded test that started this whole mess.

So, when I'm out doing the groceries and I stroll past the 'feminine hygiene' products, I do some mad calculating in my head and come to the conclusion that I'm now about fifteen weeks late.

*Fifteen weeks.*

How is this possible? How did I not realise? Am I going through early menopause? Have I been more stressed than I thought?

I pull out my phone and scroll through the calendar, double checking my workings.

Yip. Fifteen weeks late.

# Frazzled

The test had been negative. I took several to be sure. So if I'm not pregnant, then what the hell is wrong with me?

Have I mentioned my over-active imagination? I'm the kind of person who always thinks of the worst-case-scenario. I like to think it prepares me for when the worst actually does happen, but really it just sends me into an unnecessary panic.

Now that I have thoughts of cancer and the likes running through my head, I find it hard to concentrate on the rest of the groceries. I give up and head home with only a handful of what we really needed.

My mind is racing, and I put the groceries away in a daze. I need to know what's wrong with me, before I go crazy with worry. So, I pick up the phone and dial the doctors' surgery.

"Hello? I'd… like… to… make-an-appointment!" I blurt out as hot tears run down my cheeks.

"Are you alright? Is it an emergency?" the nurse asks, her voice full of sympathy.

"I… I… I don't know!" I cry and mumble something about cancer.

"Okay, hang on, I'll see what I can do." The line goes quiet as she clicks a few buttons. "I can fit you in at 3:00 pm. Can you wait until then?"

"Y-yes. Th-thank you." I hang up and drag my sleeve across my eyes, blotting out my misery.

"What's wrong, Mummy?" Ellie asks from the doorway. I freeze. I had been so caught up in my distress that I hadn't even noticed her watching me. Her wide eyes stare up at me, her bottom lip quivering.

# Frazzled

"Nothing, honey. Mummy's fine." I rush to her, sweeping her into my arms and holding her tight.

"Why were you crying? Are you sad?"

"I… ah… I just hurt myself. That's all."

"Is that why you made a pointment?" she asks.

"Ah… yeah. I just need to have a check-up."

"Like Doc McStuffins?"

I smile. "Yeah, like Doc McStuffins."

**Ellie** and Zoe keep me distracted for the rest of the afternoon, and I manage to keep my paranoia to a silent roar. My eyes still drift to the clock every few minutes. Can't be late.

When it's two o'clock, I bundle the kids into the car to drop off at Carla's while I go to my appointment. I haven't told her of my panic attacks, only that I forgot I had a routine check-up to go to. If she sees the worry in my eyes, she ignores it, and for that I am thankful. If I had to explain, I would just end up a blubbering mess. Again.

I pull up at the surgery, trying to calm my breathing before I step out from the comfort of my car. It's damn near impossible though. My heart is pounding so hard it feels as though it will fly out of my chest.

# Frazzled

Somehow, I make my feet move and carry me inside where I wait patiently for them to call my name. My knee bobs up and down, and I pick at my nails.

I follow the nurse into the doctor's room and take a seat. I stare at the medical certificates adorning the walls and the skeletal figurines on the desk. My head snaps to attention when the door opens and in rushes the doctor.

She has a kind smile and listens sympathetically as I blather on about my missed periods and how I thought maybe I had cervical cancer or some other nasty disease of the nether regions.

"I understand your concerns," she says. "I'll just get you to pop up onto the bed so we can do an external examination." She waits for me to lie down, and then gently starts to probe my stomach. "Is any of this tender?" she asks.

"No, I don't think so." I'm so certain something is wrong that I can't even tell if I'm in pain or not.

"I see." She removes her gloves and motions for me to sit back up. "Have you considered the possibility that you could be pregnant?" she asks.

"Well, I thought I was, but I took three tests, and they were all negative. That's why I'm here. There has to be something wrong, right?"

"How long ago did you take the tests?" she asks, avoiding my question.

"About two months ago."

"And you haven't had a period since when?"

"About five weeks before then."

# Frazzled

"Okay. I know you've taken tests, but I'd just like you to take another one. I need to be able to rule that out before I do any other tests." She hands me a vial and directs me to the bathroom down the hall.

So here I am, once again, knickers around my ankles, as I pee into a jar to see if there will be one line or two.

I leave the bathroom, my pee jar held to my side as I try to hide it from other patients' view. We all know that's why you get sent to the bathroom, but we all try to hide it.

I place it in my doctor's gloved hands, and she sets it on the bench, dipping an all too familiar stick into it. She leaves it to process and washes her hands. While we wait, she takes my blood pressure and measures my height and weight. I can't stop my eyes from wandering to the stick. I know I have to wait five minutes, but it's the longest five minutes of my life.

"Let's just take a look, shall we?" she says as she scoots her chair over to the bench. She doesn't say a word, she just holds it out to me.

With a shaking hand, I reach for it. I close my eyes, take a deep breath, and peer at the stick in my hand.

Two lines.

TWO LINES!

My head flicks up to look at the doctor then back down to the stick with two distinct pink lines.

I'm pregnant.

*I'm pregnant?!*

"I'm pregnant?"

# Frazzled

I stare blankly at the doctor as she clasps my other hand. "Yes, it's a positive. Congratulations, you're pregnant."

"But... But... it was negative..." I mutter, completely shocked by this new discovery.

"You can get false negatives. It happens a lot when you've only just conceived."

"So... this is... real? I'm pregnant? I'm going to have another baby?"

"Yes. You're going to have another baby." She smiles, giving my hand a squeeze.

I stumble out of the surgery, a prescription for prenatal supplements held so firmly in my hand the pharmacist has to pry it from me.

Pregnant.

I didn't see that coming.

**Frazzled**

# The Conversation

I sit quietly at the table, a forgotten cup of coffee beside me. I'm still coming to grips with the prospect of bringing another child into the family. This was never my intention—to accidentally end up pregnant—I wanted it to be a decision we made together. Now, I just have to hope like hell that hubby will be okay with it.

Devon must sense my unease, because he has come out of his room and gathered the girls into the lounge with him. He pulls out the game Jenga, and proceeds to explain the rules in a way that they can understand. I watch as they eagerly await their turns, each yelling out a hearty chant of "Jenga! Jenga! Jenga!" every time it isn't their turn. They sound so happy, giggling together.

I feel my eyes well up at the thought that our family dynamic is going to change again, and I'm not sure if they're happy or sad tears. I had come to terms with the fact that we weren't having any more, and now, here I am, fifteen weeks pregnant. I think back over the last few weeks and realise the signs had been there, I just hadn't been paying attention—too focused on my plan to make it happen, that it never even occurred to me that it was already in motion.

# Frazzled

My emotions had been all over the place. I had been even more tired than normal. And, of course, I'd had no monthly visit. That one was kind of obvious.

All of it, though, I had put down to stress.

"Oh! Mum, did you see that?!" Ellie squeals with laughter as Devon starts building the tower of blocks back up again. "Devon pulled one out of the middle and it all fell down!"

I muster a smile for her and mumble something like, "Oh, good."

"Alright, alright. I lost that one, but just you wait!" He grins, drawing her attention back to the game. For all the Neanderthal grunts I get from him the majority of the time, he can be a real gem when he wants to be.

I really should be preparing dinner. I don't even know why I'm sulking so much. I mean, a new baby is something to be celebrated, right? I'm bringing a new baby into this world.

I rub my belly without even thinking about it. When I realise what I'm doing, I smile. I'm growing a child inside of me. *Our child.*

Hubby walks in while I'm staring at my belly in wonderment. I don't even hear him.

He clears his throat. "Whatcha doing?" he asks. I can hear the smile in his voice, and I know that things will be okay.

I look up at him, fresh tears brimming as I beam at him, my hand placed on my middle.

"Does that mean what I think it means?" he asks, moving closer to me. I can't quite figure out what the look on his face means. I simply nod, my eyes pleading with his to be okay with this. "We're having another baby?" he whispers, reaching his hands out to gently rest on my hips.

"Yeah. We are." I pause, searching his eyes for a response. "I know we weren't going to have any more, but…" I don't really know where I'm going with this.

The corners of his mouth lift slightly. "We're having another baby?" he asks again.

"Yip."

He slides his hands around to my back, pulling me in to him. He nestles his head into my neck, taking a deep breath.

"Are you okay?" I ask, biting my lip as I wait for his answer.

"I'm better than okay. We're having another baby!" he cries out, lifting me in the air, making me squeal in surprise. He sets me down and plants a kiss on my lips. "I've wanted to talk to you about having another one for a while now. I just didn't know if you'd want to, you've been so busy with the kids…"

"Wait. You wanted another one?" I ask, completely thrown by his reaction.

He sighs, running his hand through his hair. "Yeah. I've been thinking about it a lot lately."

"I wanted another one too. I just didn't know how to tell you." I smile up at him.

"I hate to break up this little snuggle fest you got going on here," Devon said, poking his head around the corner, "but did I hear you right? Are you having another baby?"

# Frazzled

I laugh, "I guess there's no hiding it now. Yes. You're going to be a big brother, again."

"That's cool, I guess." He grins, walking over to me and gingerly patting my shoulder (super affectionate like). "Congratulations? I guess."

"You'll always be my first baby," I say, pulling him in for a quick hug.

"Thanks. Can you just try and make sure this one is a boy, please? I don't know if I can handle any more girls in this house."

"You and me both, son." Hubby chuckles, winking at me over Devon's shoulder.

Have I said how much I love this man?

# Frazzled

# Acknowledgements

> Well, where do I begin? Firstly, I have to thank my wonderful children for providing me with so much material to work with. I don't know if this book would have been as good, had it not been for your antics.

> My husband, Aaron, for not complaining when you come home from work, to see me sitting at the computer instead of preparing dinner like a good little housewife. For being my sounding board. For being my rock. And, of course, for our beautiful children.

> My parents, for having me ☺ and for all your support. Thanks for believing in me. Mum, you are the original Super Mum, and I can only hope to be like you xxx

> As always, my wonderful friend and proofreader, Petrina. Thanks for making sure that I don't sound stupid! You make my writing better!

# Frazzled

➤ Dena! You were the one who first told me I should be writing these stories down. You have been my cheerleader throughout this process, and for that, I thank you.

➤ My internet sister, Shannon, for letting me harass you night and day with questions and random thoughts. For sharing your experiences with me, so we can grow together in this crazy industry!

➤ And of course, to my readers! Thank you for taking the time to read my books and making my dream a reality. I love each and every one of you!

➤ If you enjoyed reading my book as much as I enjoyed writing it, please spare a moment to write a quick review on one of my platforms. Thanks again!

# Connect With Me

http://www.staceybroadbent.weebly.com

https://www.facebook.com/StaceyBroadbentAuthor

Broadbent's Bookish Babes: https://goo.gl/FY9wQN

https://www.amazon.com/author/staceybroadbent

Goodreads: https://goo.gl/YJ6dXa

https://www.instagram.com/authorstaceybroadbent/

https://www.bookbub.com/authors/stacey-broadbent

https://vm.tiktok.com/ZSJBb5bhL/

Newsletter sign-up: http://eepurl.com/cULu_f

# Frazzled

# Other Books by Stacey Broadbent

## Standalone
Never Judge a Book
Deep Heat

## Super Mum series
Frazzled
Frazzled and Frumpy
Frazzled, Frumpy and Fabulous
Super Mum: the complete series

## Flesh-eater series
Fear the Fever
Fight the Fever

## Dark Sins Novellas
Sins of the Flesh
Mine

## Hollywood Novels
Emma

# Frazzled

## A Step in Time series
Dancing through the Storm
Dancing in Circles
Dancing with Destiny
A Step in Time: the complete series

## Short Stories and Poetry
Musings, Mournings, and Misadventures

## Anthologies
The White Ribbon Collection
Scars to your Beautiful
Witching Hour: Vices and Virtues
Key to my Heart
A Touch of Inspiration
No Place like Home
Serendipity

# Frazzled

Stacey resides in Ashburton, New Zealand with her husband and three children. She is a qualified proofreader, author, wife, mother, and self-proclaimed culinary goddess. When she's not busy writing or editing books, she enjoys reading and procrastinating on TikTok.

She absolutely loves hearing from readers, so please feel free to reach out via email, Instagram, or join her reader group, Broadbent's Bookish Babes. You can also sign up to her newsletter for up-to-date info on releases.

**www.staceybroadbent.weebly.com**